JE MCCLATCHY
McClatchy, Lisa.
Eloise and the dinosaurs /

KAY THOMPSON'S ELOISE
Eloise and the Dinosaurs

STORY BY **Lisa McClatchy**
ILLUSTRATED BY **Tammie Lyon**

Aladdin Paperbacks
NEW YORK · LONDON · TORONTO · SYDNEY

 of

ALADDIN PAPERBACKS
An imprint of Simon & Schuster Children's Publishing Division
1230 Avenue of the Americas, New York, NY 10020
Copyright © 2007 by the Estate of Kay Thompson
All rights reserved, including the right of reproduction in whole or in part in any form.
"Eloise" and related marks are trademarks of the Estate of Kay Thompson.
READY-TO-READ is a registered trademark of Simon & Schuster, Inc.
ALADDIN PAPERBACKS and colophon are trademarks of Simon & Schuster, Inc.
The text of this book was set in Century Old Style.
Manufactured in the United States of America
First Aladdin Paperbacks edition January 2007
4 6 8 10 9 7 5 3
Library of Congress Cataloging-in-Publication Data
McClatchy, Lisa.
Eloise and the dinosaurs / story by Lisa McClatchy ; illustrated by Tammie Lyon.—
1st Aladdin Paperbacks ed.
p. cm.—(Kay Thompson's Eloise) (Ready-to-read)
Summary: Philip takes Eloise to the Museum of Natural History
to learn about dinosaurs.
ISBN-13: 978-0-689-87453-6
ISBN-10: 0-689-87453-7
[1. Dinosaurs—Fiction. 2. American Museum of Natural History—Fiction.
3. Museums—Fiction. 4. New York (N.Y.)—Fiction.] I. Lyon, Tammie, ill.
II. Thompson, Kay, 1911– III. Title. IV. Series. V. Series: Ready-to-read.
PZ7.M47841375Ekd 2006
[E]—dc22
2006012229

I am Eloise.
I am a city child.

I have a tutor.
His name is Philip.
He is boring, boring, boring.

Today
Philip is taking me
to the museum.

We are going
to see the dinosaurs.

And he says,
"Please behave, Eloise."

And I say,
"Please behave, Eloise."

And he says,
"Here is a dinosaur."

Philip says,
"It is a Tyrannosaurus rex."

I say,

"It is a Tyrannosaurus rex."

Then he says,
"Please stop, Eloise."

Then I say,
"Please stop, Eloise."

And he says,
"Nanny, make her stop!"

Nanny says,
"No, no, no, Eloise!"

I skip over to
the triceratops.

My pink bow
looks just right
on his horn.

I cartwheel over to
the apatosaurus.

He needs a hat.

Philip says,
"Eloise, do not touch
the dinosaurs!"

Then Nanny says,
"Eloise,
leave the dinosaurs alone.
It is time for lunch."

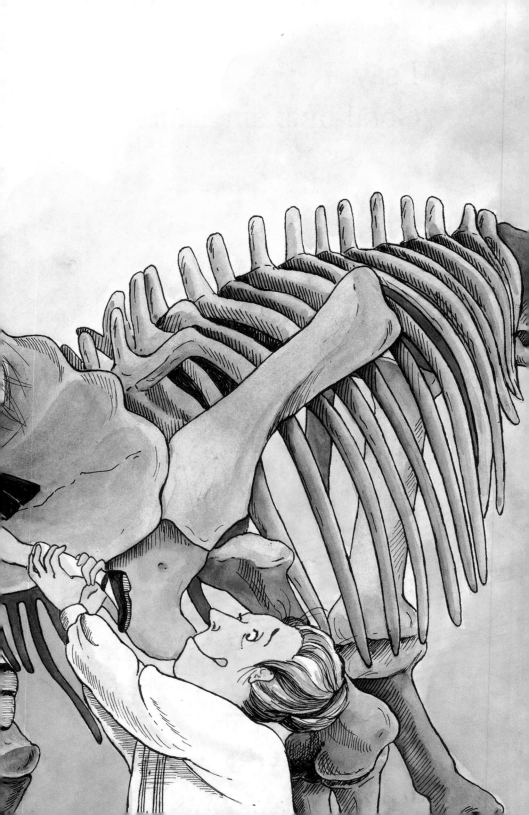

I say,
"Good-bye, dinosaurs."

Oh I love, love, love
dinosaurs!